First published in Belgium and Holland by Clavis Uitgeverij, Hasselt – Amsterdam, 2011
Copyright © 2011, Clavis Uitgeverij

English translation from the Dutch by Clavis Publishing Inc. New York
Copyright © 2012 for the English language edition: Clavis Publishing Inc. New York

Visit us on the web at www.clavisbooks.com

My Little Troublemaker written by Thierry Robberecht and illustrated by Philippe Goossens
Original title: *Mijn duiveltje*
Translated from the Dutch by Clavis Publishing
English language edition edited by Emma D. Dryden, drydenbks llc

ISBN 978-1-60537-107-8

This book was printed in September 2011 at Proost, Everdongenlaan 23,
B-2300 Turnhout, Belgium

First Edition
10 9 8 7 6 5 4 3 2 1

Clavis Publishing supports the First Amendment and celebrates the right to read

My Little Troublemaker

THIERRY ROBBERECHT & PHILIPPE GOOSSENS

Clavis

NEW YORK

At Fairy School I am never mean and I always do what is asked of me. Honestly. The teachers and the other fairies say I am the best-behaved fairy in the whole school. And I am!

Sabrina, a fairy in my class, is being really annoying today. She is making fun of me and telling everyone her dress is prettier than mine. Why is she being so mean?

I am having a hard time being nice
to Sabrina and when we are in line for
lunch, I feel like spilling soup over her
amazing dress! Oh, I so want to do that!
But I am far too well-behaved to do
something like that to anyone.

Suddenly, a tiny little fairy starts floating next to me.
She looks just like me! We're two peas in a pod!

I don't know where she's come from, but all of a sudden
that little fairy makes my hand pick up my bowl of soup
and throw it right at Sabrina!

Splash!

Oh, no! There's an enormous red-as-a-tomato stain spreading on Sabrina's dress!

"What's going on here?"
the Kitchen Fairy asks me.
"I didn't mean to do it!"
I cry, looking around for the little
fairy. She seems to have vanished.
No matter how many times
I say that it wasn't me who did it,
no one believes me.

For the first time in my life, I am being punished. The teachers make me wash all the dirty lunch dishes—without a magic wand!

After I've washed and dried a few plates and glasses, I've had enough. If only the dishes would fall and break into millions of pieces—then I wouldn't have to do the dishes anymore.

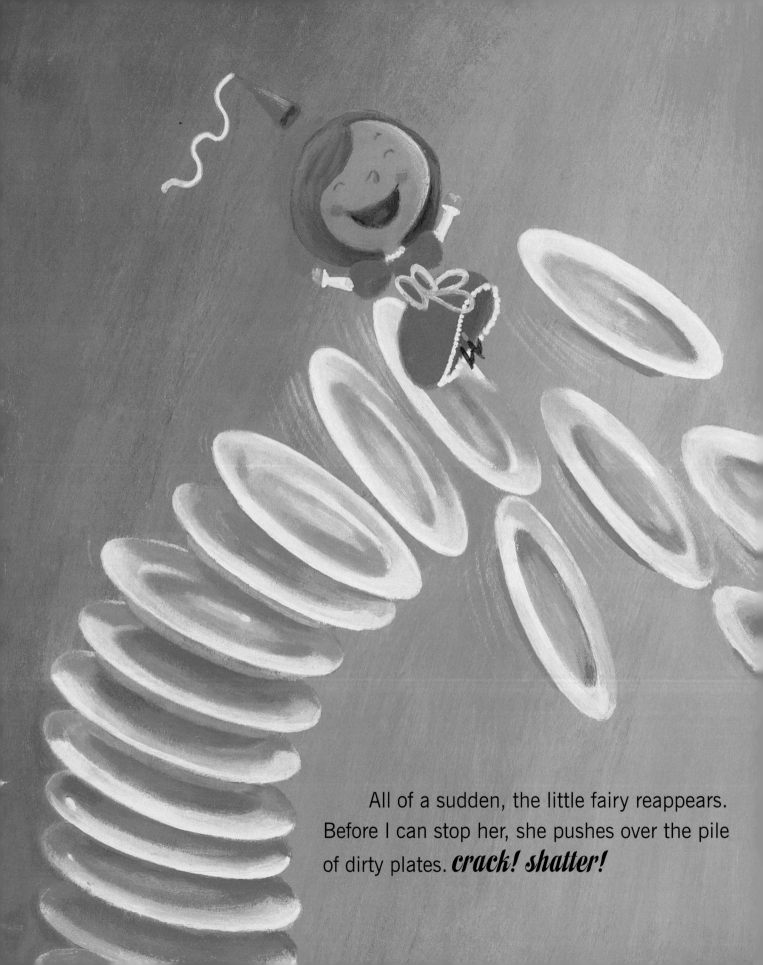

All of a sudden, the little fairy reappears. Before I can stop her, she pushes over the pile of dirty plates. *crack! shatter!*

"Oh, no! Who are you?" I cry. "Why did you do that?"
"I am your little troublemaker," the fairy replies. "I did it because you wanted to do it."

MY LITTLE TROUBLEMAKER? But that's impossible. I never do anything wrong! I need to get rid of this troublesome little fairy—and fast! I hide her in a delivery box I find in the kitchen and hurry upstairs to my room. I hope no one finds out about my secret!

Once safely in my room,
I release the little fairy.
    "Now, please tell me what
you're doing. What do you mean you
are my little *troublemaker*?"

"Well, deep in your heart you would like
to do some mean things sometimes, but you don't dare to do
so. Your little troublemaker does those things for you. You see?"

Before I can say anything else,
Sabrina bursts into my room.
  "I just *know* it was *you* who
smashed those dirty dishes," she says
with a mean laugh, "and that is what
I have told the Kitchen Fairy!"

Oh, how mean Sabrina is!
I feel like turning her into a lizard....

Just then, my little troublemaker grasps my magic wand and—*Poof!*—she turns Sabrina into a wriggly green lizard! "*Gurgle! Hiss!*" says Sabrina.

This has to stop! I have to confess everything to the Fairy Principal....

In the Fairy Principal's office I explain to her that I'm being followed by a strange little fairy who is making me do things I don't want to do.

"What does that little fairy look like?" the principal asks.

"She looks just like me, but in miniature."

"Ah, yes," the Fairy Principal says with a smile. "You have met your little troublemaker, haven't you?"

"Yes, but I don't *want* a little troublemaker!"
I plop down in a chair. "I need her to go away!"
"Oh, child," the principal says kindly,
"everyone has their own little troublemaker.
There is nothing wrong with
that because they can
sometimes help us
express our feelings.
We just have to be
careful about how
and when we ask them
to help us."
"But … Do *you* have
your own little
troublemaker too,
Fairy Principal?"

"Yes, I do. Everyone—children and adults—have them."

And suddenly I see a little fairy floating next to the Fairy Principal. They look exactly alike. Two peas in a pod!

From now on I try to be the best-behaved fairy who isn't mean and does what I'm asked to do. But every now and then, when she is really annoying me, I turn Sabrina into a lizard, frog, or a bat. Just for a short while.

I can't help it. It's not *me* who transforms her. It's my little troublemaker....